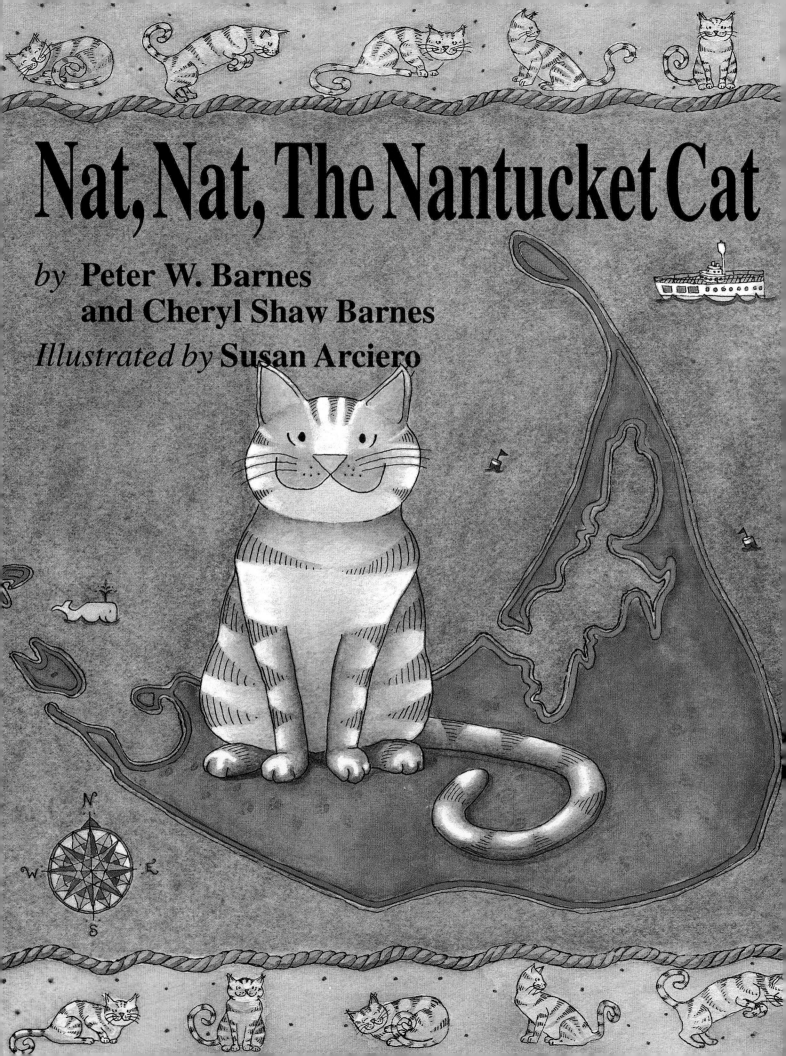

Nat, Nat, The Nantucket Cat

by **Peter W. Barnes
and Cheryl Shaw Barnes**

Illustrated by **Susan Arciero**

Other VSP books by Peter and Cheryl Barnes

Woodrow, the White House Mouse, about the presidency and the nation's most famous mansion.

House Mouse, Senate Mouse, about Congress and the legislative process.

Marshall, the Courthouse Mouse, about the Supreme Court and the judicial process.

A "Mice" Way to Learn About Government teachers curriculum guide for the three books above.

Capital Cooking with Woodrow and Friends, a cookbook for kids that mixes fun recipes with fun facts about American history and government.

Woodrow For President, about voting, campaigns, elections and civic participation.

A "Mice" Way to Learn about Voting, Campaigns and Elections teachers curriculum guide for *Woodrow for President.*

Alexander, the Old Town Mouse, about historic Old Town, Alexandria, Va., across the Potomac River from Washington, D.C.

Martha's Vineyard (with Susan Arciero), about wonderful Martha's Vineyard, Mass.

Cornelius Vandermouse, the Pride of Newport (with Susan Arciero), about historic Newport, R.I., home to America's most magnificent mansion houses.

Also from VSP Books

Mosby, the Kennedy Center Cat, by Beppie Noyes, based on the true story of a wild stage cat that lived in the Kennedy Center in Washington D.C. (Autographed copies not available.)

Order these books through your local bookstore by title,
or order **autographed copies** of the Barnes' books by calling **1-800-441-1949**,
or from our website at **www.VSPBooks.com**.

For a brochure and ordering information, write to:

VSP Books
P.O. Box 17011
Alexandria, VA 22302

To get on the mailing list, send your name and address to the address above.

ISBN 0-9637688-0-8

10 9 8 7 6

Printed in the United States of America

For our girls, Maggie and Kate,
and for Mom and Dad Barnes;
John and Michele; Tom, Lisa and CeCe;
David and Stephanie;
and anyone else who ever lived in or visited Nantucket
and fell in love with it the way we did.
—P.W.B. and C.S.B.

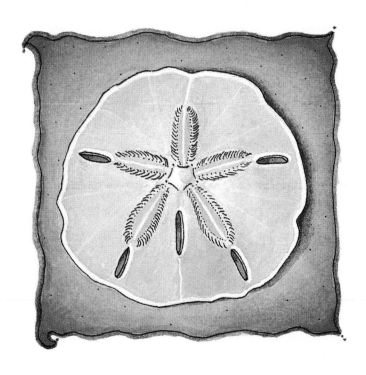

For Bill, Susan, Lucy, Pigpen,
Mom and Dad, Bruce, and Steph,
who made it all happen.
—S.A.

Nat, Nat, the Nantucket Cat,
Lives on an island that is small and flat,
Lives on an island in the deep blue sea,
And he lives so happily.

Nat, Nat, the Nantucket Cat,
  Lives with a fisherman named Captain Pat.

He fishes in the morning in the deep blue sea,
And is home in time for tea.

Nat, Nat, the Nantucket Cat,
Strolls down the street to visit Mrs. Sprat,

Down to her cottage by the deep blue sea,
Where she bakes from 8 to 3.

Nat, Nat, the Nantucket Cat,
   Sits at the window watching Mrs. Sprat,
Watching her prepare a secret recipe
   That she makes for company.

"Scat, scat, you Nantucket Cat!
    Away from my window!" bellows Mrs. Sprat.
"Away from my window, or I guarantee
    I will whale away at thee!"

Nat, Nat, a courageous cat,

Jumps

from

the window

like an acrobat,

Jumps to a sailboat in the deep blue sea,
Sailing by so gracefully.

"Nat, Nat, you amazing cat,
   Wherever are you going?" hollers Captain Pat,
Fishing by the sailboat in the deep blue sea.
   "Climb aboard and come with me!"

Nat, Nat, the Nantucket Cat,
Leaps to the Captain in a second, flat,
Leaps to his trawler in the deep blue sea,

Chugging home in time for tea.

Nat, Nat, the Nantucket Cat,
  Sleeps that very evening on the front door mat,
Sleeps on his island in the deep blue sea,
  And he sleeps so peacefully.

Historical Notes for Parents and Teachers

Nantucket Island was formed in the Great Ice Age, from sand, pebbles and stone deposited by melting glaciers. The first inhabitants were Native Americans—the island's name is derived from an Indian word meaning "the far away land." It was settled in the mid-1600s by Massachusetts Englishmen with famous Nantucket names like Coffin, Macy and Starbuck. The island's first industry was sheepraising and spinning and weaving wool.

Then the early Nantucketers discovered whaling. Historians believe they began by harvesting beached whales, then ventured offshore in search of whales in the late 1600s. But the island grew rich and prosperous in the 1700s from the hunting of the sperm whale; this great creature produced the highest quality oil, used as fuel for lamps and in candlemaking. The magnificent mansions on Main Street and elsewhere in town stand as testaments to the great whaling era, and the stories and legends of brave Nantucket seamen later found their way into Herman Melville's *Moby Dick*.

Aside from interruptions caused by the Revolution and the War of 1812, whaling flourished in Nantucket through the mid-1800s. But by the time of the Civil War, the whaling industry was essentially dead: Kerosene had been developed as lamp fuel; sperm whales were harder to find; the Great Fire of 1846 had destroyed a third of the town and many ships and crews left the island for California in the Gold Rush. The last whaling ship sailed from Nantucket Harbor in 1869.

But soon, another industry began to take whaling's place: tourism. By the turn of the century, whaling ships had given way to steamships, captains' mansions to summer cottages. "The Season" became the main source of work and income for Nantucket, and continues to be so to this day. Despite the growth in tourism in recent years, much of Nantucket's natural beauty has been preserved, thanks to the efforts of non-profit organizations such as the Nantucket Conservation Foundation, the Nantucket Land Council, the Nantucket Land Bank and many private individuals. Today, more than 30 percent of the island is permanently preserved as open space.

Nat's Nantucket includes many real-life Nantucket landmarks, locations and characteristics. In the first drawing, for example, Nat is looking out over town from a roof "walk," an architectural feature found on many island houses. The Old Mill, a working windmill that still grinds grain, is featured on several pages, too. Cobblestone streets and small cedar-shingled cottages abound.

For more information on the history of Nat's wonderful home, contact or visit the Nantucket Historical Association and the Whaling Museum.